FOR MY GRANDCHILDREN, CAROLYN ROSE,
JACOB BOWMAN, AND AVA RAE- AND ALL OF THOSE
IN THE COMING GENERATIONS OF STORYTELLERS
-JB

FOR MY LOVES AT HOME.
NOTHING ELSE MATTERS
-DD

Reycraft Books
55 Fifth Avenue
New York, NY 10003
Reycraftbooks.com

Reycraft Books is a trade imprint and trademark of Newmark Learning, LLC.

Text copyright © 2019 by Joseph Bruchac
Illustration copyright © 2019 by Reycraft Books

Library of Congress Cataloging-in-Publication Data is available.

ISBN: 978-1-4788-6868-2

Author photo courtesy of Eric Jenks
Illustrator photo courtesy of Dale Deforest

Printed in Guangzhou, China
4401/0919/CA21901483
10 9 8 7 6 5 4 3 2 1
First Edition Hardcover published by Reycraft Books

Reycraft Books and Newmark Learning, LLC., support diversity and the
First Amendment, and celebrate the right to read.

THE POWWOW THIEF

BY JOSEPH BRUCHAC   ILLUSTRATED BY DALE DEFOREST

GOING TO THE POWWOW

Jamie Longbow opened his eyes. It was still dark outside. His light had been turned on. His sister Marie tugged at his covers.

WAKE UP, LITTLE BROTHER!

I'M NOT YOUR LITTLE BROTHER. I'M TWO INCHES TALLER. AND WE ARE TWINS.

BUT I WAS BORN TWO MINUTES BEFORE YOU!

Jamie didn't argue. No one could win an argument with his sister. She also won every game they played. Even marbles. The only things he could beat her at were running and tree climbing. Especially tree climbing. Jamie was a great tree climber.

"Come on, sleepyhead. Get up. Get dressed or Grama and Grampa will go to the powwow without you."

Jamie threw off the covers and stood up. He was already dressed. "I know," he said. "I *am* ready!"

3

The twins helped their grandparents load the van. Grampa Longbow had loaded the tables and chairs and blankets. But there were lots of other things to carry. Grama Longbow made great things to sell. They carried out baskets made of ash and sweetgrass. Boxes filled with beadwork. Bags stuffed with silver and shell earrings.

Jamie knew his sister was a good reader. *She is better than me,* he thought. *She never forgets anything she reads.*

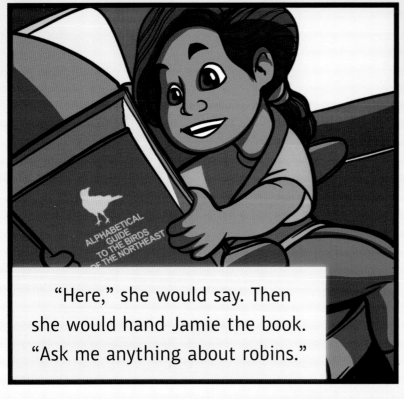

"Here," she would say. Then she would hand Jamie the book. "Ask me anything about robins."

And she always knew the answer.

A GOOD READER

When they arrived at the Little Eagle powwow grounds the sun had just risen. Lots of other Native families were there already. Setting up tents and opening up their vans. Putting out tables and covering them with blankets. Grampa knew their spot. It was the same place they came every year.

Marie put down her book. It was so exciting to be here. She saw cabinets of jewelry being unloaded. Silver, turquoise, coral, jet. Dresses and shirts made of deerskin. Blankets with wonderful designs. Rainbow-colored beadwork. Drums and rattles. Moccasins and wood carvings. Others were bringing out their regalia. So much to see!

Then the two of them started helping their grandparents set up.

They didn't hurry. They had plenty of time. Other Native vendors came to say hello. They all seemed to like Grama and Grampa a lot. They were friendly to Jamie and Marie, too.

ALPHABETICAL GUIDE TO THE BIRDS OF THE NORTHEAST

"Will do," Grampa said.

Sleepy Mickey nodded. Then he shook hands with Marie and Jamie before moving on.

"Why is he called Sleepy Mickey?" Jamie asked.

Grampa chuckled. "He can fall asleep anywhere. Once I saw him fall asleep halfway through eating a buffalo burger."

Partway through setting up, Grama looked up at the sky.
"Marie," she said, "what is that?"

Jamie shaded his eyes. A big bird flew over them. It
looked as if it was on its way toward the woods beyond the
powwow grounds. "Is it an eagle?" he asked.

Marie watched the bird carefully. "No,
silly," she said. "That's a raven. I read all
about ravens before I got to robins."

By the time the sun was three hands high, more people had arrived. Native Americans and non-Natives. Men and women, boys and girls. Tall grown-ups and babies carried by their mothers. They came to watch the drumming and dancing, to look at and buy things the vendors were selling.

"It is going to be a good day," Grampa Longbow said.

Grama stood back and looked at their tables. In the middle of one table was Grama's best piece of jewelry. A beaded necklace with silver dangles on it. Each dangle was shaped like a different bird. It sat on a wooden stand that raised it above everything else. It shone in the sun. "Yup," Grama said. "It is going to be a perfect day."

WHO TOOK IT?

The drummers began to play. The sound of their big drum rang out like thunder. The men's voices pierced the air. It was so exciting to hear that Marie couldn't help moving her feet. Her brother bounced up and down next to her, feeling the music.

They'd all been very busy. They'd sold many things. Now, though, everyone was watching the smoke dance competition.

Marie felt a hand on her shoulder. It was Grama.

GO AHEAD. YOU KIDS DID ENOUGH FOR NOW. GO ENJOY THE DANCING.

Jamie and Marie ran to the powwow circle. People packed all around it. But they could still see the dancers. Just in time. They saw the final round of smoke dancing.

"Friendship dance now," the emcee called out.
"Everyone is welcome in the circle."

The twins entered through the gate. They began dancing in the circle. All kinds of people danced. Some of the non-Natives did not know the right steps. But that was okay. Everyone was having fun.

"Look," Jamie said, pointing with his chin ahead of them. Grampa and Grama Longbow were in the circle, too. Dancing and smiling.

Who is watching our booth? Marie thought.

Grampa answered her question before she could ask it.

"It's okay," Grampa said as he danced past them. "Sleepy Mickey is watching the booth."

They only danced one song. Then all four went
back to the booth.

Sleepy Mickey was there. But he wasn't watching.
He lay slumped in his chair. Snoring. Marie and
Jamie started to laugh. But then Grama gasped.

The twins looked at the middle of the table. The wooden stand stood empty. Grama Longbow's best necklace had been stolen!

"How could someone come and take the necklace without being seen?" Jamie asked.

"And my cookie," Sleepy Mickey added. "I only took one bite out of it."

"Maybe it got knocked off the table," Jamie said. He got down on his knees and searched the ground.

Marie crossed her arms and tapped her chin with one finger. "Let me think," she said.

Jamie looked at the place where Sleepy Mickey's cookie had been. "Look," he said. "There are crumbs here and on the ground. Maybe a squirrel took the cookie and the necklace."

"I haven't seen any squirrels near here," Grampa said.

The three of them, Grama, Sleepy Mickey, and Jamie, followed Marie. She walked across a broad field until she came to the woods. She stopped below a big tree.

"Can you climb this?" she asked Jamie.

"Easy," he said.

"Do you have any marbles in your pocket?"

"A few," he said.

"Good. Leave them in exchange."

Jamie climbed the tree. Near the top sat a big nest. He looked inside and nodded.

When he came back down, he handed Grama her shiny necklace.

MY BIG SISTER WAS RIGHT. IT WAS UP THERE.

HOW ABOUT MY COOKIE?

NOPE. THE RAVEN MUST HAVE EATEN THAT BEFORE TAKING THE NECKLACE.

Soon they were back at the booth.

"How did you know the raven took that necklace?" Grampa asked Marie. She picked up her bird book and opened it. "See, right here. It says that ravens like to take shiny things."

ALPHABETICAL GUIDE TO THE BIRDS OF THE NORTHEAST

"They sure do," Jamie said. "There was a bunch of shiny things in that nest—soda cans, tinfoil."

"And now the four marbles you left in exchange for Grama's necklace," Marie added.

"Marie," Grama Longbow said, "we are proud of you."

"We sure are," Jamie said. "You are a real detective, Big Sister. You just solved the Case of the Powwow Thief."

Meet
JOSEPH BRUCHAC

I'm a writer and traditional storyteller. An enrolled member of the Nulhegan Band of the Abenaki Nation, I've performed as a storyteller and sold books and my own crafts at northeastern powwows since the early 1980s. My family and I run the annual Saratoga Native American Festival in Saratoga Springs, New York. One of my favorite powwow memories is when I was honored with a blanket at the Shelburne Museum powwow in Vermont twenty years ago.

Meet
DALE DEFOREST

I was born in Tuba City, Arizona, but raised on the Navajo Reservation in northwestern New Mexico. My mother says I've been an illustrator since I was able to hold a crayon. I used to lie on my back and draw pictures under the coffee table in my parents' living room. Apart from being an illustrator, I'm a storyteller, graphic designer, and musician. I reside in Albuquerque, New Mexico, and am a happily married father of two. Anything and everything I do, I do for my loved ones. The ultimate goal of my career is to do what I do, from the comfort of my home. Several of the characters depicted in this adorable story were inspired by loved ones in my own life, namely my mother, sister, and brother.